To Emily Frances: Sleep snug, little bug —M. E. R.
To Den, my snuggle bug —S. L.

Text © 2004 by Michael Elsohn Ross.
Illustrations © 2004 by Sylvia Long.

Book design by Sara Gillingham.
Typeset in Mramor.
The illustrations in this book were rendered in watercolor.
Manufactured in China.

Library of Congress Cataloging-in-Publication Data
Ross, Michael Elsohn, 1952-
Snug as a bug / by Michael Elsohn Ross ; illustrated by Sylvia Long.
p. cm.
Summary: Illustrations and short, rhyming verses portray bedtime rituals,
from stories to goodnight kisses, of various bugs as they settle down on
a branch, in an old cap, or under a rock and head to dreamland.
ISBN 0-8118-4245-2
[1. Bedtime–Fiction. 2. Insects–Fiction. 3. Stories in rhyme.]
I. Long, Sylvia, ill. II. Title.
PZ8.3.R7432Sn 2004
[E]–dc22
2003014121

Distributed in Canada by Raincoast Books
9050 Shaughnessy Street, Vancouver, British Columbia V6P 6E5

10 9 8 7 6 5 4 3 2

Chronicle Books LLC
85 Second Street, San Francisco, California 94105

www.chroniclekids.com

Snug As a Bug

chronicle books · san francisco

written by Michael Elsohn Ross • illustrated by Sylvia Long

It's time for a kiss.
It's time for a hug.
Get ready to sleep
as snug as a bug.

Stretch out your legs
on a soft, silky web.

Curl up in comfort
in a red, rosy bed.

Lounge in luxury
on a cool couch of green.

Fall into a fluttery
butterfly dream.

Sneak a neat nap
in an old wooly cap.

Snooze away softly
in a puddle of sap.

Cuddle in a huddle
in a grove of tall trees.

Slumber under lumber
or a blanket of leaves.

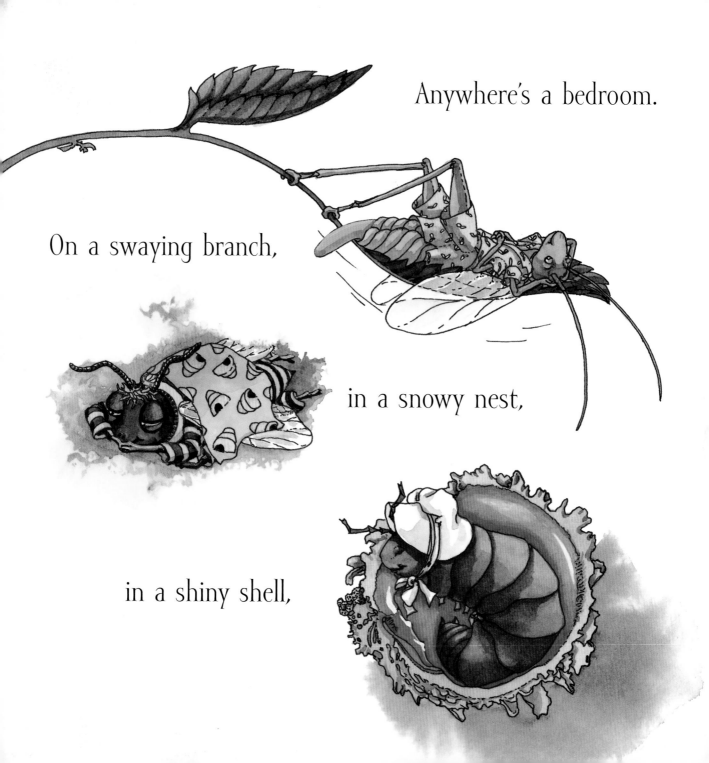

Anywhere's a bedroom.

On a swaying branch,

in a snowy nest,

in a shiny shell,

on a gorilla's big toe,

on a dirty old sock,

or under a rock.

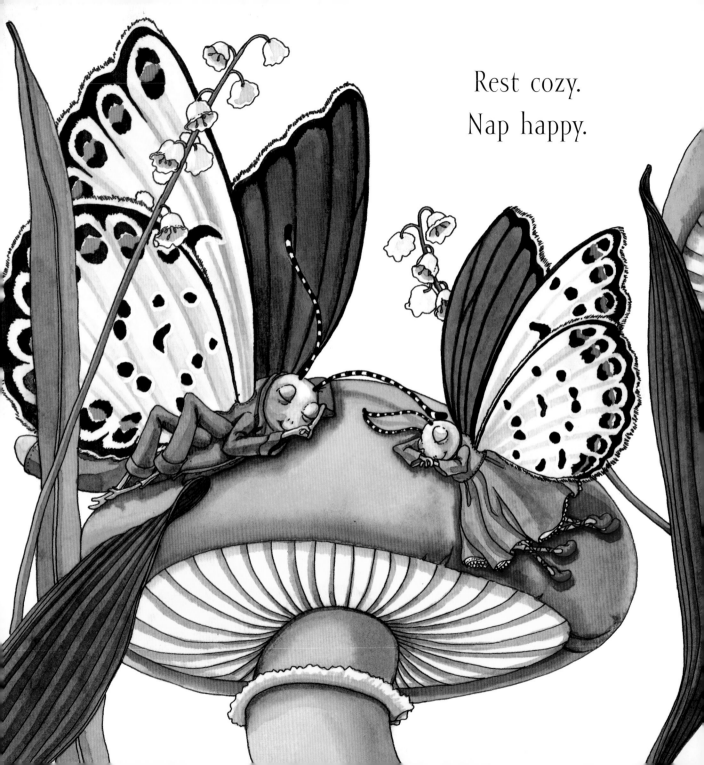

Rest cozy.
Nap happy.

Dream like a slug.

Get ready to sleep
as snug as a bug.